Bear Wants More

Karma Wilson

illustrations by Jane Chapman

SIMON AND SCHUSTER

London New York Sydney Toronto New Delhi

To my husband and best friend, Scott,

who loves my cooking so much, he always wants more

—K. W.

For Tim and Noah, with love

—J. C.

SIMON AND SCHUSTER

First Published in Great Britain in 2003 by Simon & Schuster UK Ltd

1st Floor, 222 Gray's Inn Road, London, WC1X 8HB

A CBS Company

Originally published in 2003 by Margaret K. McElderry Books,

an imprint of Simon & Schuster Children's Publishing Division, New York

This paperback edition published in 2004

Text copyright © 2003 by Karma Wilson

Illustrations copyright © 2003 by Jane Chapman

The rights of Karma Wilson and Jane Chapman to be identified as the author and illustrator of this work

have been asserted by them in accordance with the Copyright, Design and Patents Act, 1988

All rights reserved, including the right of reproduction in whole or in part in any form

The text of this book is set in Adobe Caslon

The illustrations were rendered in acrylic paint

A CIP catalouge record for this book is available from the British Library upon request

ISBN 978-1-4711-7457-5

Printed in China

1 3 5 7 9 10 8 6 4 2

When springtime comes,
in his warm winter den
a bear wakes up
very hungry and thin!

He waddles outside
and roots all around.
He digs and he paws
fresh shoots from the ground.

He nibbles on his lawn
till the last blade is gone.
But
the bear
wants more!

Mouse scampers by
with his acorn pail.
"Come along," Mouse squeaks,
"to Strawberry Vale!"

So up Mouse hops
onto Bear's big back.
They tramp through the woods
for a fresh fruit snack.

The berries grow sweet, and they eat, eat, EAT!

But
the bear
wants more!

The noon sun glows,
when along hops Hare.
"Good day, friend Mouse!
How do, friend Bear?"

"I'm HUNGRY!" roars Bear.
Hare says, "Follow me!
There's a fresh clover patch
by the cottonwood tree."

They nibble on their lunch, with a crunch, crunch, crunch!

But
the bear
wants more!

Badger shuffles by
with his new fishin' pole.
"There's a fine fish feast
at the ol' fishin' hole."

They head to the pond
and they sit by the shore.
Bear catches fish,

Meanwhile . . .
back at the big bear's den
wait Gopher and Mole
with Raven and Wren.

They bake honey cakes.
They decorate the lair.
It's a springtime party
for their good friend Bear!

Bear rubs at his tummy.
He smells something YUMMY . . .

and he still
wants
more!

Bear sniffs and he snuffles
as a sweet breeze blows.
He romps to his home.
He follows his nose.

His friends yell "SURPRISE!"
when he gets to his den.
But Bear is SO big
that he can't fit in!

Bear wails, "What luck! I am
STUCK, STUCK, STUCK . . .

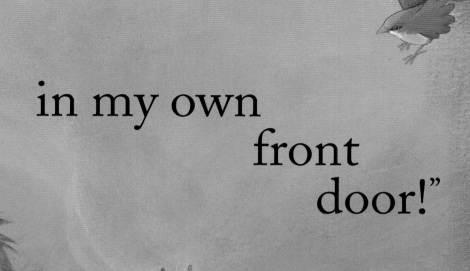

in my own
front
door!"